Postman Pat
and the
Greendale Bus

Story by **John Cunliffe**   *Pictures by* **Joan Hickson**
From the original Television designs by **Ivor Wood**

Hippo Books
in association with André Deutsch

Mrs Goggins was reading the *Pencaster Gazette* and she was looking very cross. When Pat came in for the letters, she said, "Just look at this, Pat! It says here that they're going to stop our bus service."

"They're not, are they?" said Pat. "That's terrible. How are we going to do our shopping in Pencaster without a bus? There's plenty of people haven't got a car, and Sam can't bring everything on his van."

4

"And what about when we need new glasses, or we go to the dentist?" said Mrs Goggins. "I don't know what we're going to do."

The post-office door went *ping* and Dr Gilbertson came in for some stamps.

"We'll be in a mess without a bus," said Pat. "Morning, Dr Gilbertson."

"What's all this about our bus?" said Dr Gilbertson. "Have you seen the *Pencaster Gazette*?"

"We certainly have," said Mrs Goggins. "I was just telling Pat about it."

"Well, something will have to be done," said Dr Gilbertson.

"Whoever heard of such a thing? Greendale can't manage without a bus!"

"I know," said Pat. "Why don't we get a bus of our own?"

"Hm, that's an idea," said Dr Gilbertson. "But who would drive it, and mend it when it breaks down?"

"I'll have a word with Ted," said Pat.

"And where are we going to get the money?" said Dr Gilbertson.

"I'll have a word with the Reverend," said Pat.

"And who's going to advertise it?" said Dr Gilbertson.

"I'll have a word with . . ."

"You can put a notice in my window," said Mrs Goggins.

"And who's going to get a licence?" said Dr Gilbertson. "I'll see to that myself. And I'll have a word with Councillor Moss. He's sure to help. He does anything I ask since I cured his gammy leg. Oh, yes, and I'll put a box in my waiting-room to collect money. And I'll . . ."

"Great!" said Pat. "We'll have a bus before you can say General Post Office! I'd best be on my way, now. I'll pass the word round. Cheerio!"

Pat was on his way. Everywhere he called, he told people about the plans for Greendale's very own bus service. Everyone wanted to help. He called at Greendale Farm.

"What a smashing idea," said Mrs Pottage.

"We'll paint a poster," said Katy and Tom.

Pat called at the church.

"The Lord helps those who help themselves," said the Reverend Timms. "Now the best way to raise money is to hold a garden party, with cake stalls, and a tombola, and bingo. Pick a good day and you'll get lots of people coming from Pencaster. They can't resist Granny Dryden's cakes, and Miss Hubbard's honey. You can use the vicarage garden with pleasure."

"Thanks, Reverend," said Pat.

9

At Thompson Ground, Dorothy said, "I'll make some scones and biscuits for the garden party, and let me know if there's any other help you need."

When Pat called on Ted, he said, "I've seen just the thing, down at Blackpool. I was looking for spares for the Land-Rover, and I saw this lovely old bus for sale. It was a beauty. It'll need a bit of fettling, mind. But it was a real beauty. Vintage. They don't make them like that nowadays! We'll pop down on Saturday afternoon and have a proper look. We can stop and see the cricket, after."

"Right," said Pat. "You're on."

Pat and Ted went to Blackpool in Ted's Land-Rover. Ted parked outside BILL'S BARGAIN BANGERS near the tower.

"I hope he hasn't sold it," said Ted.

But the old bus was still there, amongst the rows of second-hand cars, in a corner right at the back. Better still, it had a large notice on the windscreen saying,

REDUCED FOR QUICK SALE
PRICE ON APPLICATION

"That means he'll be glad to get rid of it," said Ted. "We might get a bargain."

Ted looked all over the bus. He wriggled underneath it. He opened the bonnet to look at the engine. He rocked it from side to side to test the springs.

Pat got in to test the seats. They were so comfortable that he fell asleep in the back.

Then Ted went to ask for the keys, so that he could try the engine. It started the second time he tried, and woke Pat up with a start.

"Runs like a bird," said Ted. "Lovely."

Bill came to see what they were doing.

"What do you reckon?" he said.

"It's a bit rough," said Ted. "It'll need a lot of work."

"Like a run?" said Bill.

"Thanks," said Ted.

"Great!" said Pat.

Bill sat in the back, and fell asleep.
They drove along the sea front at
Blackpool. The sea breeze blew through
the bus and blew all the cobwebs away.
Everyone turned to look at the old bus.

An elderly couple put their hands out at a
bus stop, and Ted stopped and gave them
a lift to the post office. They were
surprised when he didn't want their fares.
Pat and Ted had a lovely ride, and then
Ted said, "We'd better get back, and see
if we can make a bargain with Bill when
he wakes up."

Bill wasn't bothered.

"I need the space," he said. "It takes too much room up. I could get four cars in there, and they'd sell in a week. You can have it for six hundred."

"Make it five," said Ted.

"Right," said Bill. "Five hundred."

"We'll need time to get the money," said Ted.

"You've got till next Saturday," said Bill. "It'll be seven hundred after that."

"Right," said Ted. "We'll be back."

What a busy week that was in Greendale!
Only seven days to raise £500! Goodness,
what a rush!

By Tuesday, Dorothy Thompson's
kitchen was full of cakes and scones and
biscuits. Pencaster has a market on
Wednesday, and she could sell them
there, on the W.I. stall.

"They'll raise a good few pounds," she
said.

And Miss Hubbard had dozens of jars
of honey and bottles of rhubarb wine
ready for the same stall.

The children in the school made all kinds of posters, advertising

THE GREENDALE BUS BONANZA

to be put in shop windows all over Pencaster.

19

Granny Dryden was busy knitting woolly jumpers to sell at the garden party.

Alf Thompson was making walking sticks.

Peter Fogg was making corn dollies.

Everybody did something.

Thursday came, and there was a meeting in the village hall. Pat and Miss Hubbard counted all the money that had been collected.

"We have one hundred and fifty pounds, and fifty-three pence," said Pat, "including a most generous donation from Colonel Forbes."

"Magnificent!" said the Reverend Timms.

"But not enough," said Miss Hubbard. "Not half enough."

"We'll never do it in time," said Alf. "I always said . . ."

"I know what we need," said Dr Gilbertson.

"Three hundred and forty-nine pounds, and forty-seven pence," said Ted, tapping at his new calculator. "And we need it by Saturday. In two days from now."

"And I know where we can get it," said Dr Gilbertson.

"*WHERE?*" everybody said.

BusFund five pounds £5.00

"We can borrow it from the bank," said Dr Gilbertson, smiling. "I knew Councillor Moss would come in useful. He's not only on the council, he's the manager of the NatWest in Pencaster. I'll pop in and see him first thing tomorrow. Don't worry. I'll see to it. And we'll have months to collect the rest of the money and pay it back."

"When we get the bus on the road," said Ted, "we'll be able to use part of the fares to pay the money back."

"And we'll have time to organise a really good garden party," said the Reverend Timms.

"And I'll have time to knit lots of jumpers for the stall," said Granny Dryden. "I ran out of wool last night."

"Great!" said Pat.

Dr Gilbertson came back on Friday with
a cheque for five hundred pounds.

"He said we'd need extra for petrol and
the licence," she said. "Isn't he good?"

On Saturday, Pat and Ted went for the bus. They drove it back to Greendale, and parked in the village for all to see.

"It needs a good clean out," said Mrs Goggins. "Just look at that floor. And the windows can't have been washed for years."

"And it'll need new covers on the seats," said Miss Hubbard. "They're worn out."

"And it needs rubbing down and repainting," said Sam. "The way I did my van. It'll look like new. I've got some paint left over."

"I'll have that engine stripped down," said Ted.

"But it's a lovely bus," said Pat, and they all agreed with that.

So Greendale was busy again. Cleaning, and polishing, and painting, and oiling every part of that old bus. Making new seat covers. Planning routes. Making more posters. Getting tickets printed. Going to the bank. Filling in forms. There was something for every single person to do. Even baby Paul helped to make a poster.

When all was finished, you never saw
such a bus in all your life. There never
was a bus like the Greendale bus! Every
seat had its own hand-made cover, and a
pretty cushion. The bus gleamed with
new paint and polish. It was better than
new.

Then there was a problem.

"Who's going to drive it?" said Dr Gilbertson.

"I'd like to drive it," said Ted. "I like driving buses."

"Yes," said Dr Gilbertson, "but you need a special licence to drive with paying passengers on board."

"Oh," said Ted. "I didn't know that."

"Oh, dear," said the Reverend, "what are we going to do?"

Now they had a bus, but no driver. But when Pat called on Miss Hubbard with her letters, and told her about the problem, she laughed, and said, "But didn't you know, Pat?"

"Didn't I know what, Miss Hubbard?" said Pat.

"Well, I drove a bus during the war, in Preston! *And* I've kept my licence up. Here it is! I'll just need a bit of practice on my own, and off we go! I love driving a bus."

And so it was that Miss Hubbard was the first driver of the Greendale bus. For some days, she went slowly along the wider roads in the bottom of the valley, and practised turning and backing on the village green where there was plenty of room.

Nobody said anything about a few
scrapes on the paintwork here and there,
which were quickly painted over by Ted.
But she soon got into the way of it, and
edged out on to the main road to
Pencaster, and even had a trip up the
motorway. When it was time for the bus
service to begin, she was an expert bus
driver once more, and even gave Ted
some lessons.

"We must have an opening ceremony," said the Reverend Timms. And so they did. The Pencaster Silver Band came to play.

The Pencaster Morris Men danced
on the village green.

Crowds came from Pencaster, and from even farther away, on that sunny Saturday. They put a lot of money in the collecting boxes. And they filled every seat in the bus for its first run.

"All aboard for the Blackpool trip!" shouted Sam.

And off they went, with Miss Hubbard at the wheel.

It was a great run. People waved to them all the way to Pencaster. The Greendale bus was quite famous now. It was in the papers, and filmed for television. With bus services closing down all over the country, people thought it was a marvellous idea.

They had a good time at Blackpool. They paddled in the sea, went on the pier, and had big fluffy pink swirls of candyfloss.

Before they went home, they called round
at BILL'S BARGAIN BANGERS to
show him how his bus was getting on.

He wouldn't believe it was the same bus, until Pat lifted a seat cover to show him the seat underneath.

"Well, I'll be blowed," said Bill. "I reckon it's worth a thousand or two, now."

"But we're not selling it," said Pat. "Not ever."

"You never know," said Ted. "We might be needing another one in a bit."

Then off they went, home to Greendale,
tired and happy.

The proper Greendale bus service started on Monday, and it's been going ever since. Ted takes turns at driving it with Miss Hubbard, and Peter Fogg's having lessons. It's often full, or nearly full. You can hear Miss Hubbard calling out, "Room for one more if you all squash up a bit!"

She'll always fit you in, somehow.